VET'S ORDERS

Story by Mary Risk

illustrations by The County Studio

HEINEMANN · LONDON

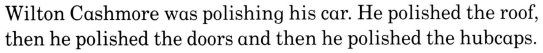

Wilton Cashmore was polishing his car. He polished the roof, then he polished the doors and then he polished the hubcaps.

Spanner came to take a look. He leaned against the bonnet.

"Watch out!" barked Wilton. "You'll mark the paintwork!"

Fiona whizzed up on her bike.

"Mind that puddle!" said Wilton. "You'll splash the wheel!"

Wilton was bending over the last hubcap when the *Delilah* arrived. Joshua Jones and Fairport jumped ashore.

"I'd better go before Josh wants me to help him," said Spanner. "See you later."

Fairport liked cars. He trotted through a patch of mud and started sniffing round the front of Wilton's car. He could hear Wilton, but he couldn't see him.

To get a better look, Fairport jumped up on the bonnet.

Wilton straightened up. He saw Fairport. Then he saw Fairport's paw marks. He went bright red.

"Oi!" he exploded. "Get off there! Dratted dog!"

Fairport wagged his tail. He wasn't used to being shouted at.

"Now look here," began Josh.

Wilton took a step forward. He didn't see the sponge. He slipped. The polishing rag shot out of his hand. It flew through the air and whizzed past Fairport's ear.

Fairport gave a yelp of surprise, and slithered backwards off the bonnet onto the ground. He landed heavily on one of his back legs.

"Here boy! Come here!" called Josh.

Fairport slowly limped towards him.

Josh bent down to pat him, then stood up. He was angry.
  "You had no right to do that, Mr Cashmore," he said.
  Wilton looked ashamed.
  "Yes, but look at those paw marks," he said. "My car ..."
  "Bother your car," said Josh. "My dog ..."

Fiona was bending over Fairport. She looked up.

"I think he's hurt himself Josh. He's limping badly."

Wilton's face grew paler.

"Oh dear," he said. "I didn't mean ... I hope he's ..."

"This is a job for Daphne," said Josh. "You'd better come with me, Fiona. You can look after him till we get there."

It seemed a long way to Daphne's cottage. Josh steered the
Delilah up the canal at full speed. Fiona settled Fairport in his
basket and tucked a blanket over him. Fairport tried to stand up,
but he whined and lay down again.

"Good dog," said Fiona. "You just stay quiet. We're nearly there
now. Daphne will know what to do, won't she Josh? Daphne's a
really good vet. I'm going to be a ..."

Josh smiled at her.

"I know. You're going to be a vet one day. And seeing the way
you're looking after poor old Fairport, I'd say you're going to be a
good one."

When they reached the lock, Josh carried Fairport up the path
towards Daphne's surgery.

Daphne was outside her cottage, inspecting her car's engine.
   "I'll just tighten this up a bit, and … Yes, it'll do now."
   Josh came up with Fairport in his arms.
   "Can you take a look at Fairport, Daphne? He's hurt."
   "Fairport? What happened?"
   "Daddy lost his temper," said Fiona, feeling embarrassed.
"And Fairport slipped, but Daddy didn't mean to hurt him."
   "I'm sure he didn't," said Daphne. "Let's take a look."

Very gently, Daphne ran her hands over Fairport's leg.

"Hm, a fracture, I'm afraid. It's not bad and it will heal very quickly. But we'll have to put the leg in plaster. And Fairport will need to keep very quiet for the rest of today. I'll keep him here with me."

"I don't know about that," said Josh.

"Joshua Jones," said Daphne, "no arguing! Vet's orders!"

At Biggott's Wharf, Wilton sat in his office. He tried to work.
He couldn't. He tried to tidy his desk. He couldn't.

"I'm never going to lose my temper again," he said.

Spanner came in. He banged the door open too hard.

"You great twit ..." began Wilton. He stopped.

"Yes, Mr Cashmore?"

"Er, nothing. Have a tea break, Spanner. You look hungry."

Spanner's mouth dropped open.

"Feeling all right, are you, Mr Cashmore?"

"Yes. Perfectly all right." Wilton stood up. "I'm going out.
I've got to see a man about a dog. I mean a woman. I mean a vet."

He went outside and jumped in his car.

Daphne was getting ready to set Fairport's leg.

"Can I help, Daphne? Please!" said Fiona. "I'll be very, very careful. I'll do everything you say. I'll ..."

"Your first job, Fiona, is to stop talking! Your second is to stand beside me and hand me things when I ask for them. Now Josh, keep Fairport still. I'm going to give him an injection. He won't know a thing about this."

Daphne worked quickly. Fiona and Josh helped her. None of them saw a face peeping in at the window.

"Oh dear," said Wilton to himself. "It looks very serious. And it was all my fault. Poor Fairport! Whatever can I do to help him get better?"

He tiptoed away.

Later, Fairport opened one eye. Then he opened the other. Then he opened his mouth and gave a huge yawn. He stood up and looked round at his leg in surprise. It was covered with thick white plaster.

Daphne laughed. "He'll soon get used to it," she said. "And it's only for a week or two. That leg will be as good as new."

"How are you going to look after him here, Daphne?" said
Fiona. "I mean, you've got to go out to all your other patients.
Won't you need someone to help you?"

"I believe I will. And I think I know just the person."

"Do you mean ...?" Fiona looked hopeful.

"Yes, I do. You've been a very good nurse this morning.
Very good indeed."

"Hear, hear," said Josh. "I'll see you in a few minutes. I'm going
outside for some fresh air."

It seemed quite easy looking after Fairport. Fiona put bowls of food and water in Daphne's comfortable dog-pen. Then the phone rang.

"Emergency at Grimspool," said Daphne. "I've got to go. You'll have to hold the fort, Fiona."

She got into her car, and went off with a clatter and a bump.

For the first few minutes, nothing much happened.
"This is easy," thought Fiona.
Then a cat went past the window. Fairport barked at it.
"No, Fairport!" said Fiona. "You're meant to be resting!"
Suddenly, the telephone rang. Fiona answered it.
"Vet's surgery? Oh hello, Mr Laski. Is there a message?"
She was writing the message down when the doorbell rang.

Wilton stood on the doorstep. He was carrying a large bone.

"How is he?" he said.

Fiona laughed. "He's fine Daddy, really," she said.
"Come and see."

Fairport saw the bone and barked happily.

"Oh dear," said Fiona. "I don't think he ought to have that yet.
He's not supposed to get excited."

Wilton crept out of the room.

Out in the lane, he bumped into Josh. Wilton went pink.

"Ah, Mr Jones. Yes – well – I – that is – I'm sorry."

"It's all right, Mr Cashmore. I know you didn't mean to hurt Fairport. It was an accident."

"Yes, and I'm never going to lose my temper again."

He dived into his car and pulled something out.

"I've got a present for you," he said.

"A budgie," said Josh. "Well I never. I'll take it back to Grimspool with me."

Daphne drove up. She nearly bumped into Wilton's car.
  "Hey!" he yelled. "You blithering ... Oops!" He stopped.
  Fiona ran out of the surgery.
  "Thank goodness you're back, Daphne. Joe Laski phoned.
One of his piglets is in trouble."

"A piglet? I'll go at once," said Daphne.

She tried to start her car again. It wouldn't start. She got out and opened the bonnet.

"Oh no!" she groaned. "This time it's serious."

"You can take her, can't you, Mr Cashmore?" grinned Josh.

"Go to a farm? In my car?" burst out Wilton. He caught Josh's eye. "Oh, all right then," he said.

Up at the farm, Joe Laski was waiting for them.

"He's very small, Miss Peacock," he said. "I think he needs medicine."

Daphne looked at the piglet carefully.

"So do I," she said. "Come along, young fellow. A high-class ambulance service for you!"

"A pig? In my car?" said Wilton. "Certainly not! He'll mess up the seats. He'll eat the gear lever. He'll …"

"Don't worry, Mr Cashmore," said Daphne. "I'll hold him on my knee. Pigs are really very clean, you know."

Soon they were almost back at the cottage.

"Phew!" said Wilton, wiping his forehead. "I'm glad that's over. Goodbye! Must be getting back to the office!"

But Fiona was waiting on the doorstep.

"Daphne! Thank goodness you're back!" she said. "A sheep is trapped in a ditch. It's stuck in the mud."

"Right," said Daphne. "You look after the piglet, Fiona. Mr. Cashmore, back in the car. You can't go home yet, I'm afraid."

"First a pig, now a sheep!" groaned Wilton. "This is terrible!"

The sheep was well and truly stuck.

"I'll push, and you pull," said Daphne to Wilton as she stepped into the water. "One! Two! Three …!"

With a loud sucking noise, the sheep shot out of the mud.

"Well done, Mr Cashmore," said Daphne. "You've got quite a way with animals."

Wilton tried to look modest. He nearly succeeded.

At the surgery, Fiona was looking hot.

"Here you are at last!" she said to Daphne. "The phone's rung twice, and the doorbell's rung three times, and Fairport's upset his water ..."

"That's life – for a vet," said Daphne. "How is Fairport?"

"Look!" said Fiona.

Fairport was looking much better. He barked with excitement when he saw Wilton.

"He's ready for his bone, now," said Fiona.

She fetched the bone. Fairport chewed it happily.

"He loves it, Daddy," she said.

"Of course he does," said Wilton. "I knew what he'd like. I understand animals, you know."

The telephone rang again. Wilton answered it.

"Yes, of course, Mr Biggott. At once, Mr Biggott."

He put the phone down.

"Mr Biggott needs me. I must get back straightaway."

"Going back to the wharf, eh?" said Daphne. "Josh is there. You can take Fairport back to him. He's well enough now."

Back on the *Delilah*, Fairport trotted straight into the cabin to find his basket. Then he saw the budgie.

"Woof!" he barked crossly. "Grr!"

"I don't think he's too pleased," said Josh. "Tell you what, Fiona, why don't you keep the budgie for me?"

"Oh yes!" said Fiona. "Can I, Daddy?"

"A budgie?" said Wilton. "All that noisy chirping? Certainly not." He saw Josh winking at him. "Oh – er – well, yes, all right, Fiona!"

First published in Great Britain 1993
by William Heinemann Limited
an imprint of Reed Children's Books
Michelin House, 81 Fulham Road, London SW3 6RB
and Auckland, Melbourne, Singapore and Toronto

ISBN 0 434 96222 8

Printed and bound in Italy
by OFSA - Milano